In memory of my wonderful Oba-chan.
(With thanks to Annie, Gracey, Rachael, and Jackie.) —K.M.

To warm soapy bodies and bits, scrubbed clean, steamy and free —G.Z.

Visit us on the Web! rhcbooks.com
Educators and librarians, for a variety of teaching tools, visit us at RHTeachersLibrarians.com

Library of Congress Cataloging-in-Publication Data
Names: Maclear, Kyo, author. | Zhang, Gracey, illustrator.
Title: The big bath house / Kyo Maclear ; illustrated by Gracey Zhang.
Description: First edition. | New York : Random House Studio, [2021]
Audience: Ages 4–8. Audience: Grades K–3. | Summary: Soon after a young girl arrives in Japan,
she, her grandmother, her aunties, and some cousins celebrate cultural traditions together
while visiting a bath house.
Identifiers: LCCN 2020049264 (print) | LCCN 2020049265 (ebook) | ISBN 978-0-593-18195-9
(hardcover) | ISBN 978-0-593-18196-6 (lib. bdg.) | ISBN 978-0-593-18197-3 (ebook)
Subjects: CYAC: Bathhouses—Fiction. | Family life—Japan—Fiction.
Racially mixed people—Fiction. | Japan—Fiction.
Classification: LCC PZ7.M2246 Big 2021 (print) | LCC PZ7.M2246 (ebook)
DDC [E]—dc23

The text of this book is set in 18-point BelleMT Pro.
The illustrations were rendered in ink, gouache, and watercolor paints.
Book design by Rachael Cole

MANUFACTURED IN CHINA
10 9 8 7 6 5 4 3 2 1
First Edition

Baachan: short for Oba-chan, or "Grandmother" in Japanese

Geta: a Japanese wooden sandal

Ma anata wa okiku narimashita ne: My, you've grown so big

Shizukani: quiet

Yukata: a light cotton kimono worn during the summer or after a bath

THE BIG
BATH HOUSE

WRITTEN BY Kyo Maclear ILLUSTRATED BY Gracey Zhang

RANDOM HOUSE STUDIO • NEW YORK

When you get to Baachan's place,
you'll forget about all the time that's passed
and everything that happened to get you there.

You'll tumble toward her and she'll shuffle toward you, and it'll be understood.

The wooden sandals will be lined up and waiting,
and you'll know the aunties are coming—
the aunties with their big stories and bigger purses.

They'll rush toward you
and you'll inch toward them,
and it'll be understood.

Ma anata wa okiku narimashita ne . . .

You'll walk down the street,
your aunties sounding like clip-clopping horses,
geta geta geta,
in their wooden sandals,

and the warm wind will rustle
through your yukata.

Until you arrive . . .

at the bath house.

The big bath house.

To the bath that is steaming.
To your cousins, all beaming.

The water will flow
and the garden will grow
at the big bath house.

The birds will be fed
and your clothes will be shed
at the big bath house.

Note by note, the chimes will ring.
Tune by tune, a voice will sing
at the big bath house.

But first comes washing.

Baachan's stool is a throne.
She is the Queen of the Baths.
With a tall towel crown,
she'll wash your hair,

while the aunties scrub each other's backs.
And the big bath waits.

You'll do the soapy leg
can-can—
soapy hands,
soapy knees.

You'll do the wood barrel
drumroll . . .

until it's time.

Then,

little by little,
side by side,

you—your baachan, aunties, and cousins—

will slip into
the big bath.

A chorus of one long breath:

Soak it up, sink right in.
Into the tub.
The steaming tub
in the big bath house.

You'll all dip your bodies,
your newly sprouting,
gangly bodies,
your saggy, shapely,
jiggly bodies,

your cozy, creased,
ancient bodies.

Beautiful bodies.

After the bath, your auntie's arms will open wide,

and you'll be wrapped up snug in a soft cloud.

While you're waiting for Baachan and the aunties,
you'll find big chairs for flopping
and sweet shaved ice for slurping.

Then you'll say goodbye to the bath house.
The big bath house.

Face flushed, you'll walk
into the cool night air.

You'll walk through the quiet, glowing streets.

Hush, the aunties will say. *Shizukani.*

The houses are sleeping.

They are so pretty when they sleep.

We don't want to wake them.

You'll reach for Baachan's hand, and she'll reach for yours.

And it'll be understood.

(Some things just go without saying.)

Someday you'll find the words,
but for now,
you have this.

This day at the big bath house.

AUTHOR'S NOTE

As a child, I spent July and August in Japan, at my grandmother's house. The moment I arrived, I stepped into a world of love and soaked it all in—the warm grassy smell of tatami mats, the comforting sight of house slippers lined up by the front door, and the familiar clatter of teacups as the family gathered to greet my mother and me. My grandmother and I didn't share a common language, but we shared rituals, a sweet tooth, and a love of bathing! Every summer, we would take a trip to the neighborhood bath house with all my female relatives and raise the roof with our chatter and laughter. During our long soaks, I would feel the distance of a year dissolve. This story, close to my heart, was inspired by my childhood memories of "Baachan."

Because of the bath house, I grew up surrounded by naked bodies of all ages, shapes, and sizes. I saw breasts of women who had nursed many babies. Large bottoms, saggy bottoms. Grandmas with gentle rolls of fat. The idea that bodies should always be private and clothed wasn't the norm, and part of my hope with this story is to share and celebrate this other way of being.